THIS WALKER BOOK BELONGS TO:

_____

_____

_____

This collection first published 1997 in *The Three Little Pigs* and *Hey Diddle, Diddle*
by Walker Books Ltd, 87 Vauxhall Walk, London SE11 5HJ

This edition published 2004

2 4 6 8 10 9 7 5 3 1

Illustrations © 1997 Jane Chapman

The right of Jane Chapman to be identified as illustrator of this work
has been asserted by her in accordance with the Copyright,
Designs and Patents Act 1988

This book has been typeset in ITC Highlander

Printed in China

All rights reserved.
No part of this book may be reproduced, transmitted
or stored in an information retrieval system in any form
or by any means, graphic, electronic or mechanical,
including photocopying, taping and recording,
without prior written permission from the publisher.

British Library Cataloguing in Publication Data:
a catalogue record for this book is available
from the British Library

ISBN 1-84428-829-3
www.walkerbooks.co.uk

Jane Chapman

Sing a Song of Sixpence

A Pocketful of Nursery Rhymes and Tales

WALKER BOOKS
AND SUBSIDIARIES
LONDON · BOSTON · SYDNEY · AUCKLAND

Contents

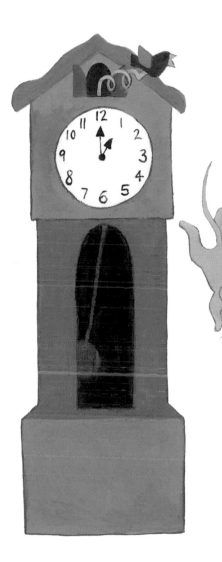

Mary Had a Little Lamb

Mary had a little lamb,
Its fleece was white as snow;
And everywhere that Mary went
The lamb was sure to go.

It followed her to school one day,
That was against the rule;
It made the children laugh and play,
To see a lamb in school.

And so the teacher turned it out,
But still it lingered near,
And waited patiently about
Till Mary did appear.

Why does the lamb love Mary so?
The eager children cry;
Why, Mary loves the lamb, you know,
The teacher did reply.

The Queen of Hearts

The Queen of Hearts
She made some tarts,
All on a summer's day;
The Knave of Hearts
He stole the tarts,
And took them clean away.

The King of Hearts
Called for the tarts,
And beat the knave full sore;
The Knave of Hearts
Brought back the tarts,
And vowed he'd steal no more.

Pussy Cat, Pussy Cat

Pussy cat, pussy cat,

Where have you been?

I've been to London

To look at the queen.

Pussy cat, pussy cat,

What did you there?

I frightened a little mouse

Under her chair.

Humpty Dumpty

Humpty Dumpty sat on a wall,

Humpty Dumpty had a great fall.

All the king's horses and all the king's men,

Couldn't put Humpty together again.

Jack and Jill

Jack and Jill
Went up the hill,
To fetch a pail of water;
Jack fell down,
And broke his crown,
And Jill came tumbling after.

The Three Little Pigs

Once upon a time there was an old mother pig who had three little pigs. As she was too poor to keep them, she sent them out to seek their fortune.

The first little pig set off, and he met a man with a bundle of straw. "Please, Sir," said the first little pig, "give me that straw to build a house," which the man did, and the first little pig built his house.

No sooner had he finished
when along came a wolf
and knocked at the door.
"Little pig, little pig, let me
come in," said the wolf.

And the little pig answered,
"No, no, no! Not by the hair
of my chinny chin chin!"
So the wolf said,
"Then I'll huff
and I'll puff
and I'll *bloooow*
your house in!"

And the wolf huffed and he puffed and he blew
the house in, and ate up the
first little pig.

The second little pig met a
man with a bundle of sticks.
"Please, Sir," said the
second little pig, "give me
those sticks to build a house,"
which the man did, and the
second little pig built his house.

No sooner had he finished when along
came a wolf and knocked at the door.

"Little pig, little pig, let me come in," said
the wolf. And the little pig answered,
"No, no, no! Not by the hair
of my chinny chin chin!"

So the wolf said, "Then I'll huff and I'll
puff and I'll *bloooow* your house in!"

18

And the wolf huffed and he puffed,
and he *puffed* and he *huffed*, and
at last he blew the house in,
and ate up the second
little pig.

The third little pig met a
man with a load of bricks.
"Please, Sir," said the
third little pig, "give me
those bricks to build a house,"
which the man did, and the
third little pig built her house.
No sooner had she finished when along
came a wolf and knocked at the door.
"Little pig, little pig, let me come in,"
said the wolf. And the little pig answered,
"No, no, no! Not by the hair of my chinny
chin chin!"
So the wolf said, "Then I'll huff and
I'll puff and I'll *bloooow* your house in!"

And the wolf huffed and he puffed,
and he *puffed* and he *huffed*,
and he **huffed**
and he **puffed**,

but he could not blow the house in.

Then the wolf was very angry indeed and said he would come down the chimney and eat up the little pig.

So the third little pig made a blazing fire, and put a huge pot of water on to boil. Just as the wolf was coming down the chimney, the little pig took the lid off the pot, and in fell the wolf.

Then the little pig put the lid back on again, boiled up the wolf until nothing was left of him, and lived happily ever after.

Little Bo-peep

Little Bo-peep has lost her sheep,
And doesn't know where to find them.
Leave them alone, and they'll come home,
Bringing their tails behind them.

Baa, Baa, Black Sheep

Baa, baa, black sheep,

Have you any wool?

Yes, sir, yes, sir,

Three bags full:

One for the master,

And one for the dame,

And one for the little boy

Who lives down the lane.

Three Blind Mice

Three blind mice! Three blind mice!

See how they run! See how they run!

They all ran after the farmer's wife,

Who cut off their tails with a carving knife,

Did you ever see such a thing in your life,

As three blind mice?

Hickory, Dickory, Dock

Hickory, dickory, dock,

The mouse ran up the clock.

The clock struck one,

The mouse ran down,

Hickory, dickory, dock.

Mary, Mary, Quite Contrary

Mary, Mary, quite contrary,
How does your garden grow?
With silver bells and cockle shells,
And pretty maids all in a row.

Little Miss Muffet

Little Miss Muffet
Sat on a tuffet,
Eating her curds and whey;
There came a big spider,
Who sat down beside her
And frightened Miss Muffet away.

Goldilocks and the Three Bears

Once upon a time there were three bears who all lived together in a little house in the forest. There was a great big Daddy Bear, a middle-sized Mummy Bear and a little tiny Baby Bear.

One morning the three bears made a pot of porridge for their breakfast, but it was too hot to eat.

"Let's go for a walk in the forest," said Mummy Bear. "When we get back, the porridge will have cooled."

Not long after the three bears
had left, a little girl with golden
hair came up to the house.
Her name was Goldilocks.
She knocked on the door
three times. When no one
answered, she tried the handle
and to her surprise the door opened.
Goldilocks walked in and went
straight over to the table.
"Oh, porridge! My favourite!"
she said.

First Goldilocks tasted the
porridge in the great big bowl.
"Ugh, much too salty!" she said.

Then she tasted the
porridge in the
middle-sized bowl.
"Ooh, much too
sweet!" she said.
Last of all she tasted the porridge
in the tiny baby bowl. "Mmm,
just right!" said Goldilocks
and she ate it all up.

Goldilocks felt very full, so she went into the sitting-room, where there were three chairs. First she sat on the great big chair.

"Ow, much too hard!" she said.

Then she sat on the middle-sized chair.

"Ooh, much too soft!" she said.

Last of all she sat on the tiny baby chair.

"Ahh, just right!" sighed Goldilocks.

But – CRACK! – the tiny baby chair broke into pieces and Goldilocks fell on to the floor.

Now Goldilocks felt tired.
She went upstairs to the
three bears' bedroom.
First she lay down on
the great big bed.
"Ooh, much too
high!" she said.

Then she lay down on the middle-sized bed.
"Ugh, much too lumpy!" she said.
Last of all she lay down
on the tiny baby bed.
"Ahh, just right!"
said Goldilocks
and she went
straight to sleep.

Soon the three bears came back from their walk.

They were all very hungry.

Daddy Bear looked at his great big bowl.

"Who's been eating *my* porridge?"

he said in his great

big voice.

Mummy Bear looked at her middle-sized bowl.
"Who's been eating *my* porridge?" she said
in her middle-sized voice.
Then Baby Bear looked
at his tiny baby bowl.
"Who's been eating
my porridge?" he cried
in his tiny baby voice.
"And has EATEN IT
ALL UP!"

The three bears went into the sitting-room.
Daddy Bear turned around to sit in his chair.
"Who's been sitting in *my* chair?" he said in
his great big voice.

Mummy Bear looked
at her chair.
"Who's been sitting
in *my* chair?"
she said in her
middle-sized voice.
Then Baby Bear looked
at his chair.

"Who's been
sitting in my
chair?" he cried
in his tiny baby
voice. "And has
BROKEN IT
ALL TO BITS!"

The three bears ran upstairs to look in their bedroom.

"Who's been sleeping in *my* bed?" said Daddy Bear in his great big voice.

"Who's been sleeping in *my* bed?" said Mummy Bear in her middle-sized voice.

Then Baby Bear looked at his bed.

"Who's been sleeping in my bed?"

he cried in his tiny baby voice.

"And IS STILL THERE!"

Goldilocks woke up and was very frightened

to see the three bears all looking down at her.

She leaped out of bed, jumped straight out

of the window and ran

home as fast as

she could.

And the three bears never saw her again.

Sing a Song of Sixpence

Sing a song of sixpence,
A pocket full of rye;
Four and twenty blackbirds,
Baked in a pie.

When the pie was opened,
The birds began to sing;
Wasn't that a dainty dish,
To set before the king?

The king was in his counting-house,
Counting out his money;
The queen was in the parlour,
Eating bread and honey.

The maid was in the garden,
Hanging out the clothes;
When down came a blackbird,
And pecked off her nose.

There Was an Old Woman

There was an old woman who lived in a shoe,

She had so many children she didn't know what to do;

She gave them some broth without any bread;

She whipped them all soundly and put them to bed.

There Was a Crooked Man

There was a crooked man,
And he walked a crooked mile,
He found a crooked sixpence
Against a crooked stile;
He bought a crooked cat,
Which caught a crooked mouse,
And they all lived together
In a little crooked house.

Yankee Doodle

Yankee Doodle came to town,

Riding on a pony.

He stuck a feather in his cap

And called it macaroni.

Ride a Cock-horse

Ride a cock-horse to Banbury Cross,
To see a fine lady upon a white horse;
Rings on her fingers and bells on her toes,
And she shall have music wherever she goes.

The Little Red Hen

Once upon a time there was a little red hen
who lived in a farmyard with a dog, a cat and
a goose. One day the little red hen found
some grains of wheat.

"Who will help me plant this wheat?" she asked.

"Not I!" said the dog.

"Not I!" said the cat.

"Not I!" said the goose.

"Then I shall plant it myself,"
said the little red hen.

And she did.

The wheat grew and grew and when summer
came, it turned golden yellow in the sun.
Now it was ready to be harvested.
"Who will help me cut this wheat?"
asked the little red hen.
"Not I!" said the dog.
"Not I!" said the cat.
"Not I!" said the goose.
"Then I shall cut it myself,"
said the little red hen.

And she did.

Now the wheat needed to be threshed,
to separate the hard husks from the grain.
"Who will help me thresh this wheat?"
asked the little red hen.
"Not I!" said the dog.
"Not I!" said the cat.
"Not I!" said the goose.
"Then I shall thresh it myself,"
said the little red hen.

And she did.

Now the grain was ready to go to the mill, to be ground into flour.

"Who will help me carry this grain to the mill?" asked the little red hen.

"Not I!" said the dog.

"Not I!" said the cat.

"Not I!" said the goose.

"Then I shall carry it myself," said the little red hen.

And she did.

The miller ground the grain into flour, ready for baking and the little red hen carried it home.

"Who will help me bake this flour into bread?" asked the little red hen.

"Not I!" said the dog.

"Not I!" said the cat.

"Not I!" said the goose.

"Then I shall bake it myself," said the little red hen.

And she did.

When the bread was baked to a golden brown,
the little red hen took it out of the oven.
A delicious smell drifted over the farmyard.
"Who will help me eat this bread?"
asked the little red hen.

"I will!" said the dog.

"I will!" said the cat.

"I will!" said the goose.

"Oh no, you won't!" said the little red hen.

"I shall eat it all myself!"

And she did . . .

right down to the very last crumb.

Polly Put the Kettle On

Polly put the kettle on,
Polly put the kettle on,
Polly put the kettle on,
We'll all have tea.

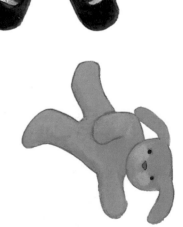

Sukey take it off again,
Sukey take it off again,
Sukey take it off again,
They've all gone away.

Pat-a-cake

Pat-a-cake, pat-a-cake, baker's man,

Bake me a cake as fast as you can;

Pat it and prick it, and mark it with B.

Put it in the oven for Baby and me.

Hey Diddle, Diddle

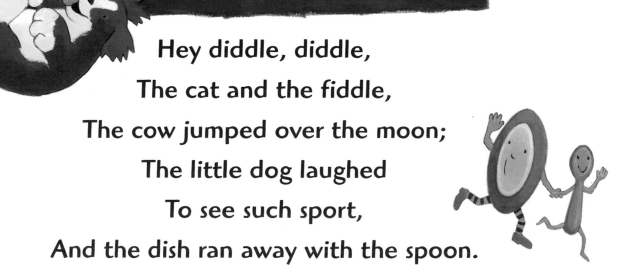

Hey diddle, diddle,

The cat and the fiddle,

The cow jumped over the moon;

The little dog laughed

To see such sport,

And the dish ran away with the spoon.

Jack Be Nimble

Jack be nimble,
Jack be quick,
Jack jump over
The candlestick.

Wee Willie Winkie

Wee Willie Winkie runs through the town,
Upstairs and downstairs in his nightgown,
Rapping at the window, crying through the lock,
Are the children all in bed, for now it's eight o'clock?

Twinkle, Twinkle, Little Star

Twinkle, twinkle, little star,

How I wonder what you are!

Up above the world so high,

Like a diamond in the sky.

Twinkle, twinkle, little star,

How I wonder what you are!

WALKER BOOKS is the world's leading
independent publisher of children's books.
Working with the best authors and illustrators
we create books for all ages, from babies
to teenagers – books your child will
grow up with and always remember. So…

FOR THE BEST CHILDREN'S BOOKS,
LOOK FOR THE BEAR